Lincoln Peirce

BiG NATE
LAUGH-O-RAMA

HARPER
An Imprint of HarperCollinsPublishers

ISBN 978-0-06-211116-6

Typography by Andrea Vandergrift
14 15 16 17 18   CG/RRDH   10 9 8 7 6 5 4 3 2 1
❖
First Edition

For Big Nate Fans All Over the World—
Especially if you love…
cartooning,
laugh attacks,
Cheez Doodles,
scribble games, and
green beans (Okay, forget that last one.)

POP QUIZ PARTY!

Are you a Big Nate know-it-all? Prove it!

1. Who has a crush on Nate?

   a. Spitsy

   b. Kim Cressly

   c. Maya

   d. Dee Dee

2. When Randy steals a camera away from Nate and tosses it up in the air, who catches it?

   HA HA HEH HEH HAW!

   a. Chad

   b. Teddy

   c. Gina

   d. Nick Blonsky

3. What instrument does Mary Ellen Popowski play?

   a. drums

   b. harp

   c. flute

   d. guitar

4. This is Gina's Trivia Slam team name.

a. Gina's Gorgeous Brains

b. Gina's Gonna Get You

c. Gina's Geniuses

d. Gina's Great Gamers

5. Francis DOESN'T do this:

a. color code his underwear

b. iron his tube socks

c. speak in baby talk to his cat

d. get a C on his homework

BONUS POINTS!

When Uncle Pedro hypnotizes Nate, he becomes . . .

a. funnier

b. a world-class guitarist

c. neat

d. a hip-hop dancer

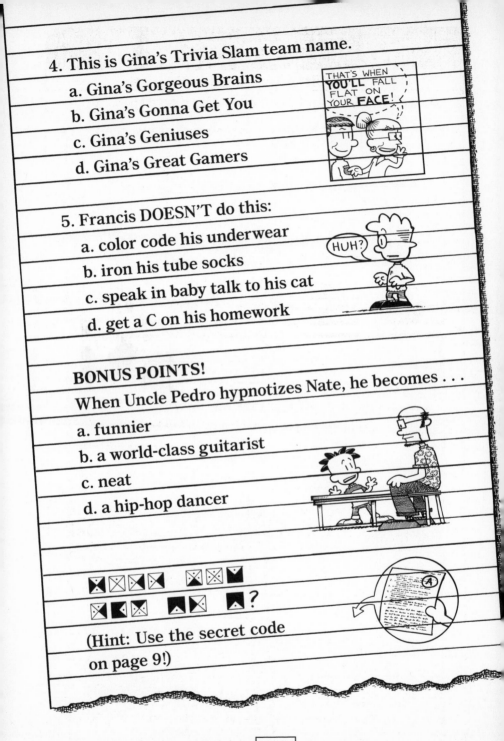

(Hint: Use the secret code on page 9!)

GOTCHA!

Have you ever had a bad-picture day? Take a look at these silly shots! Make up a crazy caption for each one.

_____

_____

_____

_____

NOW DRAW YOUR OWN
<u>WEIRDEST</u> PHOTOS EVER!

WALK
THE PLANK

Nate's friend Chad wears his favorite pirate hat during the Trivia Slam showdown. How well do you know pirates? Try this puzzler and see!

CLUES

ACROSS

2. The glistening gold and jewels that pirates seek.

5. How pirates say "Hello!" It rhymes with "boy."

6. The leader of the sailors.

8. A vessel that travels on the high seas.

9. A replacement for a pirate's hand; rhymes with "cook."

10. Tall, brown, and leather, these will keep your feet warm.

DOWN

1. What pirates say when they're angry; the last three letters are the same.

3. A black accessory that covers one of your eyes.

4. A wooden board that rhymes with "sank." Walk the _____.

6. This will lead you to true North.

7. Feathered friend that often sits atop one's shoulder; rhymes with "carrot."

8. Long and sharp, this weapon serves pirates in battle.

NAME THAT BRAIN!

Test your Big Nate know-how! Match each character with their favorite subjects—draw a line from each set of subjects to the right character.

science fiction, martial arts, video games

sports, comedy, foreign languages, movie quotes

NO INFO

art, drama, fashion, musical theater

every- thing ...and MORE!

GINA HEMPHILL-TOMS

ERIC FLEURY

DEE DEE HOLLOWAY

TEDDY ORTIZ

? ? ? ?

CODE CRACKER

Use this alphabet to decode the secret messages in this book. But don't show it to anybody else!

SECRET AGENT

Nate's dramatic friend Dee Dee loves playing a spy! Now you try. Decide what your secret spy identity will be. Circle your choices below.

SPY NAME: _____

(You choose!)

DISGUISE:

a. mustache and beret

b. mask and cape

c. glasses and wig

d. Halloween costume

SIDEKICK:

a. your dog

b. the pizza-delivery boy

c. a karate master

d. your crush

SECRET SYMBOL:

a. star and moon

b. lightning flash

c. diamond in a circle

d. an *X* in a square

NOW DRAW
YOURSELF IN YOUR
SPY DISGUISE!
(SHHH! DON'T TELL!)

SLAM DUNK

Who is the trivia champ of P.S. 38?

START

FINISH

HALL MONITOR

Nate can't stand Nick Blonsky, the hall monitor who always reports him. List 15 reasons Nate gets into trouble, then rank them from 1 (no sweat) to 5 (worst ever).

REASON	RANK
1.	___
2.	___
3. Running in the hall	___
4.	___
5.	___
6. Eating Cheez Doodles	___
7.	___
8. No hall pass	___
9.	___
10.	___
11. Skateboarding inside	___
12.	___
13.	___
14.	___
15.	___

UGH. NICK.

WHAT ARE YOU DOING HERE?

DRESS TO IMPRESS

THERE'S NOTHING I ADORE MORE...

OOF!

Dee Dee is a fan of fabulous outfits! Find all the clothing and accessories in the word scramble on the opposite page and help Dee Dee get dressed!

HEADBAND

SNEAKERS

DIAMOND TIARA

NECKLACES

COWBOY HAT

RAINBOW BLOUSE

SATIN GLOVES

VEST

FEATHER BOA

LEG WARMERS

EARRINGS

STRIPED SCARF

SKIRT

ARGYLE SOCKS

WILD WORDS

Teddy and Francis combined the words "slob" and "pig" to make up a new word, "SLIG"!

NOW YOU TRY:

slime + dirty =

_____

phobia + fright =

_____

dumb + chuckle =

_____

yellow + purple =

_____

stinky + old =

_____

yummy + fun =

_____

style + snappy =

_____

spice + tasty =

_____

crazy + dork =

_____

SO FUNNY!

SHORTCUT!

Nate knows a secret shortcut through Little Woods to get home from school. Check out Ms. Clarke's lesson, then turn the page to create an awesome Mad Lib about your adventure in Little Woods!

Let's review the parts of speech. What is a noun?

A noun is a person, place, or thing.

EXAMPLES:

Mrs. Godfrey (person), library (place), Book of Facts (thing)

EXAMPLES: memorize, practice, compete

EXAMPLES:

phony (Gina's smile)

snappy (Nate's comebacks)

dorky (Dee Dee's thinking caps)

And an adverb is a word that describes an adjective or a verb. Here's how to use one in a sentence: Francis is driving Nate <u>completely</u> insane.

MAKE A LIST OF THE COOLEST WORDS YOU CAN THINK OF:

1. Noun:

2. Noun:

3. Verb:

4. Noun:

5. Plural noun:

6. Adjective:

7. Adjective:

8. Verb:

9. Noun:

10. Noun:

11. Noun:

12. Noun:

13. Noun:

14. Verb:

15. Noun:

16. Adjective:

17. Verb:

18. Verb:

NOW FILL IN THE BLANKS
TO CREATE YOUR ADVENTURE!

When I enter the woods, I hear a _____
1.

and trip on a _____ , causing me to
2.

_____ quickly. As I turn up the hill, a
3.

_____ drops out of a tree and lands on
4.

my _____ . There are _____
5.   6.

noises all around, and I feel _____ .
7.

I turn to _____ when suddenly a
8.

_____ is in my path.
9.

"What's going on?" I think as I pick up the

_____ and put it in my _____ .
10.   11.

I sigh and run toward the _____
                                                  12.

when I see a _____ through the
                              13.

clearing.

I _____ loudly and sprint before
          14.

the _____ catches up. The sky turns
          15.

_____ , and I _____ through
16.   17.

the mud and _____ as fast as I can!
                          18.

22

PROBLEM PICS!

Has your school picture ever turned out <u>TOTALLY</u> terrible? Match each disaster to the right photo!

WANTED!

In *Big Nate Flips Out*, Nate suspects that sneaky Nick Blonsky stole the school camera. Draw your own WANTED posters for these characters and list their crimes. Are they too annoying? Or overly dramatic? You decide!

MAKE UP DEE DEE'S CRIME!

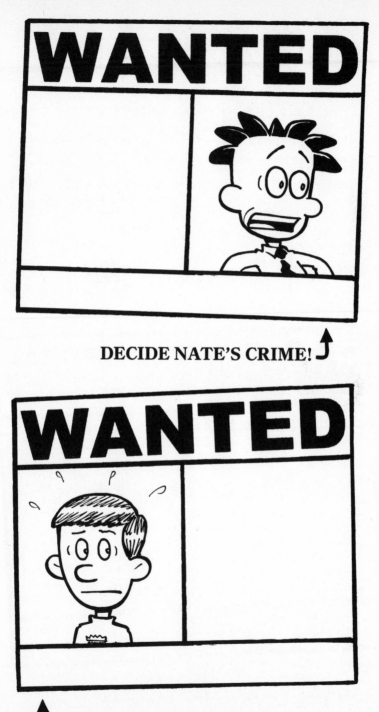

DECIDE NATE'S CRIME!

WHAT DID RANDY DO?

YOU'RE AN ACE!

Can you fill in the grid so that each card suit only appears once in every row, column, and box?

WHAT THE...?!

MASTERMIND MATCHUP

It's Trivia Slam time at P.S. 38, and Nate's ready for a showdown! Match each of his classmates to their trivia specialty!

CHAD APPLEWHITE

every-thing

MARY ELLEN POPOWSKI

comics, Ben Franklin, history of snack foods, Greek myths

FRANCIS POPE

flute music, cosmetology, reality television

NATE WRIGHT

breakfast, scouting, lunch, animals, dinner

FACTASTIC FRANCIS

How well do <u>you</u> know Nate's best friend Francis??
Test your facts with this quick quiz!

1. Francis's favorite hobby is . . .

a. skateboarding

b. making collages

c. learning new trivia

d. climbing trees

2. Francis's nickname is . . .

a. Mr. Muscles

b. Fearless First Mate

c. General Giggles

d. Captain Tidypants

THAT'S MY NAME!

3. Francis's favorite animal is . . .

a. duck-billed platypus

b. koala

c. cat

d. gerbil

4. Francis has . . .

a. an aunt Patty

b. a baby sister

c. twin brothers

d. no siblings. He's an only child.

5. Francis's favorite household task is . . .

a. cleaning the basement

b. ironing his tube socks

c. shoveling snow

d. repairing gadgets

THAT POSTER'S NOT STRAIGHT!

DON'T TRASH IT!

RECYCLE IT!

6. Francis's dream job is . . .

a. a geologist

b. an epidemiologist

c. a farmer

d. a professional wrestler

SHOVE!

COME ON, GUYS! WE'VE GOT SCIENCE!

KNOCKOUT NOTES

Nate's notebook is filled with dramatic doodles! See if you can find all the things and people listed below and circle each one in Nate's notes on the opposite page.

BATHTUB

CLOWN

FRANKENSTEIN

SPITSY

PUPPET

BRICK WALL

LIGHTNING BOLT

KUNG FU MASTER

TIC-TAC-TOE GAME

MAD SCIENTIST

RANDY

BASKETBALL

ULTRA-NATE

DUCK

SPACESHIP

CUBE

HEART

33

GUESS WHO?

How well do you know all the cool characters in Nate's world? Using the clues, see how fast you can solve this crossword puzzle!

CLUES

ACROSS

2. Mr. Perfect and Jenny's boyfriend.

3. Nate's #1 best friend; he LOVES trivia and color coordinating his socks.

4. Know-it-all and teacher's pet, also Nate's enemy.

6. Nate's big sister (who's a little full of herself!)

7. Nate's other best friend; he's super funny and awesome at sports.

9. He teaches art, Nate's favorite class!

10. Nate's social studies teacher, also known as Godzilla.

DOWN

1. He's the boss at P.S. 38 and runs the school.

5. She's so cute that Nate's had a crush on her since first grade.

8. She's one super drama queen!

SUPER SPY

Where should Dee Dee, super spy,
look for the missing camera?

THE SCRIBBLER

Play the scribble game!

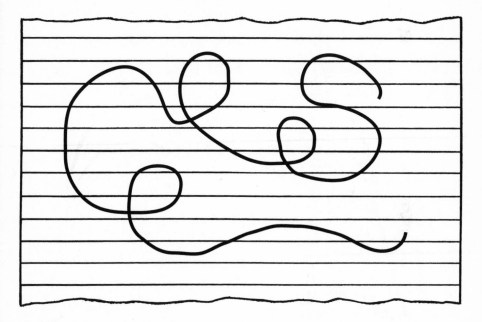

Challenge yourself! Try writing a caption with your left hand if you're right-handed, or vice versa.

CANDID CAMERA

Gina, Nate's rival, wants to be yearbook editor. Why? So that she can feature great photos of . . . guess who? GINA!

WRITE A FUNNY CAPTION FOR EACH PHOTO!

_____
_____
_____

_____
_____
_____

GAG ME!

The kids at P.S. 38 love to trade totally gross Gag Me cards, even though they aren't allowed at school! Make the most disgusting Gag Me card characters by drawing lines from List A to List B!

List A

SLIMY

FARTY

MESSY

BURPY

STINKY

SLOBBY

GREASY

GASSY

SMELLY

DIRTY

List B

GERTIE

ROBBIE

MARTY

KELLY

CASSIE

KIRBY

BESSIE

PINKY

CEE CEE

JAIME

DRAW YOUR OWN GAG ME CARDS WITH CHARACTERS AS YUCKY AS <u>SNOTTY SCOTTY</u>.

↑ WRITE YOUR
CARD NAME HERE.

THINKING CAPS

When Nate's trivia team compete, they put on their thinking caps. See if you can find all the caps listed below in the puzzle on the opposite page!

TIARA

SOMBRERO

BEANIE

SWIM CAP

BERET

BONNET

BASEBALL CAP

VISOR

BANDANNA

HELMET

FEDORA

BOWLER

FEZ

COWBOY HAT

TURBAN

TOP HAT

FASCINATOR

CROWN

BRAIN BOWL

IT'S **TRIVIA** TIME!!

Are you ready to test your brain big-time? Get ready for some totally tough trivia! Don't worry, you will surpass all others!

1. Which continent is the farthest north?

   N _ _ _ _ _   _ _ _ _ _ _ _ _

2. What insect has eight legs?

   S _ _ _ _ _ _

3. Which planet is known for its rings?

   S _ _ _ _ _ _

4. What does a caterpillar transform into?

   B _ _ _ _ _ _ _ _ _

5. Tokyo is the capital city of which country?

<u>J</u> _ _ _ _

6. What organ pumps your blood?

<u>H</u> _ _ _ _

7. What shape has three sides?

<u>T</u> _ _ _ _ _ _ _

8. What gas do we need to breathe to stay alive?

<u>O</u> _ _ _ _ _

9. What are the names of the five oceans on Earth?

<u>A</u> _ _ _ _ _ _ _ _

<u>P</u> _ _ _ _ _ _

<u>I</u> _ _ _ _ _

<u>A</u> _ _ _ _ _

<u>S</u> _ _ _ _ _ _ _

10. Where can you find the Empire State Building?

<u>N</u> _ _ _ _ _ _ _

FUNKY FITNESS

You may not think these activities are types of fitness . . . but they are! Can you fill out the grid so that each letter appears once in every row, every column, and every shaded box?

D = **DANCING**

M = **MALL WALKING**

C = **CURLING**

F = **FINGER JOUSTING**

NATE NERD

Are you an über-brain when it comes to Nate-tastic trivia? Let's see! Put that thinking cap to work, and circle either true or false for each statement.

1. Mrs. Godfrey gave Nate an A++.

☐ TRUE   ☐ FALSE

2. Chad is afraid of cats.

☐ TRUE   ☐ FALSE

3. Teddy is the lead singer in Nate's band, Enslave the Mollusk.

☐ TRUE   ☐ FALSE

4. Principal Nichols asks Nate to be a hall monitor.

☐ TRUE   ☐ FALSE

NOW GET BACK TO CLASS.

YESSIR.

5. Uncle Pedro is related to Artur.

☐ TRUE   ☐ FALSE

6. Francis has a job delivering newspapers.

☐ TRUE   ☐ FALSE

LUDWIG VAN BEETHOVEN WAS BORN IN 1770! THE STATE BIRD OF NEW HAMPSHIRE IS THE PURPLE FINCH! THE AVERAGE TEMPERATURE ON JUPITER IS −162° F! THE MOST POPULAR TV SHOW DURING 1963 WAS...

ENOUGH PRACTICING! **ENOUGH PRACTICING!!**

FACE-OFF!

Whoa! Check out these wacky faces from the candid photos in Nate's yearbook. See if you can draw the same face in the blank box next to each picture!

ROOM RAID

Take a look at Nate's bedroom—it's majorly messy! See if you can find all the items below and circle each one on the opposite page.

BANANA PEEL

SOCCER BALL

BASEBALL

BRUINS POSTER

PHOTO STRIP

BASEBALL CARD

RED SOX PENNANT

GOLF CLUBS

MONKEY STICKER

DOCTOR CESSPOOL COMIC

PORT CITY BIKES BUMPER STICKER

3 SOCKS

COMIX

SPIDER

PENCIL

DARTBOARD

SPIDERWEB

BASEBALL CAP

BOBCATS BAG

LAMP

MRS. GODFREY DRAWING

SALTY SAM'S CRACKERS

SCHOOL SCRAMBLE

Gina, the teacher's pet, sure loves school! What is Gina up to now? Draw a line from each school location to the correct photo below.

HALLWAY

SCHOOL YARD

LIBRARY

CAFETORIUM

IT'S A
WONDERFUL LIFE

Why is Nate flipping out?

PASS THAT CLASS!

What's the subject of today's class? Big Nate, obviously! Get your pencils ready—you're sure to ace this one.

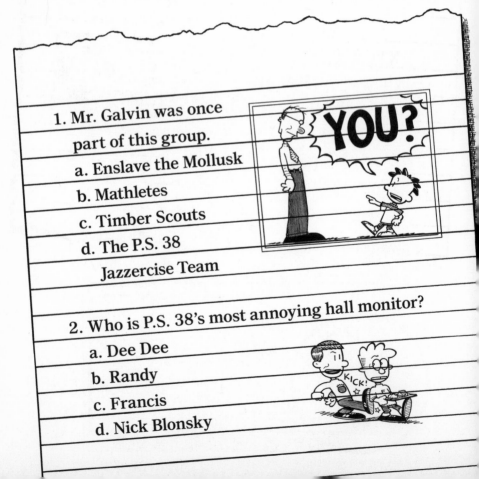

1. Mr. Galvin was once part of this group.

a. Enslave the Mollusk

b. Mathletes

c. Timber Scouts

d. The P.S. 38 Jazzercise Team

2. Who is P.S. 38's most annoying hall monitor?

a. Dee Dee

b. Randy

c. Francis

d. Nick Blonsky

3. What is Teddy's uncle's name?

    a. Uncle Francis

    b. Uncle Pedro

    c. Mr. Holloway

    d. Chad

4. Who likes to wear disguises?

    a. Spitsy

    b. Randy

    c. Artur

    d. Dee Dee

EXTRA CREDIT!

Who gets crazy about keeping

his lawn tidy?

    a. Nate's dad

    b. Mr. McTeague

    c. Mrs. Godfrey

    d. Francis

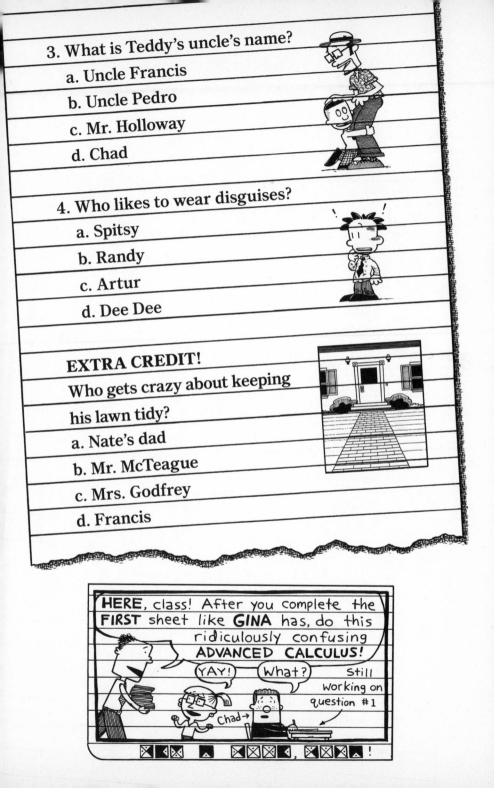

HERE, class! After you complete the FIRST sheet like **GINA** has, do this ridiculously confusing **ADVANCED CALCULUS!**

YAY!

What?

Still working on question #1

Chad →

READY, SET, CLICK

Nate wants to be a photographer for the yearbook—by taking lots of <u>crazy</u> candid photos! If you can find all the photo terms in this puzzle, you are a master behind the camera!

CANDID

CLOSE-UP

COMPOSITION

CAMERA

EXPOSURE

ANGLE

ZOOM

CROP

DARKROOM

SMILE

BACKLIGHTING

FLASH

FILM

NEGATIVES

PRINTS

SUBJECT

BULB

PHOTOGRAPHER

FOCUS

LENS

POSE

```
S  L  C  R  S  U  B  J  E  C  T  A
M  M  A  R  E  M  A  C  B  R  S  N
O  D  I  D  N  A  C  S  U  P  U  G
O  S  N  L  B  L  K  I  L  U  C  L
R  S  D  P  E  H  L  D  B  E  O  E
K  N  E  G  A  T  I  V  E  S  F  X
R  E  H  P  A  R  G  O  T  O  H  P
A  L  O  Z  P  R  H  S  A  L  F  O
D  R  O  P  L  A  T  F  P  C  M  S
C  O  M  P  O  S  I  T  I  O  N  U
M  T  C  P  R  I  N  T  S  L  S  R
R  I  A  D  H  S  G  R  P  U  M  E
```

MISERABLE MIDDLE NAMES

HAW! HEY!
BUTT HURTS!

Nate's friend Francis gets teased because his middle name is Butthurst. Poor Francis! Draw lines from List A to List B below to create the worst middle names.

List A

BUTT

SLIME

FART

DIM

BURP

DORK

GROSS

SMELL

STINK

List B

SONG

MAN

KING

WIT

US

SON

ON

IT

FAST

NOW WRITE ALL THE MISERABLE MIDDLE NAMES YOU CREATED. RANK THEM FROM 1 (EMBARRASSING!) TO 10 (CAN'T EVER LIVE IT DOWN!!!).

NAME	RANK
1.	____
2. Dorkus	____
3.	____
4.	____
5.	____
6.	____
7. Burpsong	____
8.	____
9.	____
10.	____
11. Fartman	____
12.	____
13.	____
14.	____
15.	____

FRANCIS NEEDS TO GET **OVER** HIMSELF!

THERE ARE MIDDLE NAMES **WAY** WORSE THAN THAT!

FRANCIS FACTOIDS

Can you fill in the grid so that each Francis fact only appears once in every row, column, and box?

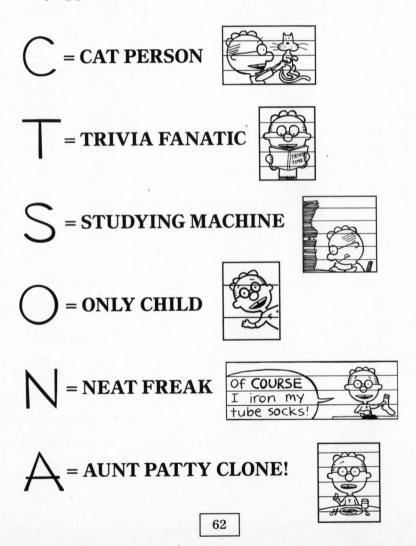

C = **CAT PERSON**

T = **TRIVIA FANATIC**

S = **STUDYING MACHINE**

O = **ONLY CHILD**

N = **NEAT FREAK**

A = **AUNT PATTY CLONE!**

Chew at least **TWENTY TIMES** before swallowing!

And then **FLOSS** after eating!

*He doesn't have a mustache like Aunt Patty, but otherwise the similarities are **UNCANNY!**

PICTURE DAY

Uh-oh! It's the School Picture Guy—watch out!
Fill in the speech bubbles and decide what happens.

WHO'S WHO?

How well do you know all the kids at Nate's school?
Draw a line from each kid to the correct name!

ERIC FLEURY

MARY ELLEN POPOWSKI

RANDY BETANCOURT

TEDDY ORTIZ

DEE DEE HOLLOWAY

GINA HEMPHILL-TOMS

FRANCIS POPE

CHAD APPLEWHITE

GIRL WHO DRAWS UNICORNS

MASH-UP MAYHEM

Quick! Make your own comic using
Coach John, a butterfly, and Dee Dee!

 +

 + =

YOUR TITLE HERE

CHEEZ, PLEASE!

CRUNCH
CRUNCH

What's Nate's all-time favorite food? Scrumptious and delicious Cheez Doodles, of course! He's even written poems about them! See if you can solve the puzzle and find all the reasons Nate goes crazy for Cheez Doodles!

CLUES

ACROSS

2. This means delicious and rhymes with "tummy"!

5. Not baked but _____, this rhymes with "hide."

6. Rhymes with "girl." The shape of the Doodle.

7. Nate's favorite after-school _____ that keeps him satisfied until dinner!

8. Rhymes with "breezy." This is the flavor that makes them so irresistible!

DOWN

1. What Nate does when he eats them—the opposite of a frown!

3. Mix red and yellow together to make this color.

4. The sound of devouring a Doodle. It rhymes with "munch."

YUMMY!

MESS-O-METER

...BECAUSE YOU'RE SO **MESSY!**

Nate's notorious for being a mess—rank these from eww to gross out!

1. Spray cheese in your socks

☐ EWW ☐ GAG ME

☐ YUCK ☐ GROSS OUT

2. Boogers on your desk

ANYBODY GOT A TISSUE?

☐ EWW ☐ GAG ME

☐ YUCK ☐ GROSS OUT

3. Moldy tuna sandwich in your locker

☐ EWW ☐ GAG ME

☐ YUCK ☐ GROSS OUT

4. Spit in the corner of your teacher's mouth

☐ EWW ☐ GAG ME

☐ YUCK ☐ GROSS OUT

5. Flies land on your burger

- ☐ EWW
- ☐ YUCK
- ☐ GAG ME
- ☐ GROSS OUT

6. Stinky six-month-old gym shorts

- ☐ EWW
- ☐ YUCK
- ☐ GAG ME
- ☐ GROSS OUT

7. Slimy bologna from last week's lunch

- ☐ EWW
- ☐ YUCK
- ☐ GAG ME
- ☐ GROSS OUT

8. Grease all over your notebook

- ☐ EWW
- ☐ YUCK
- ☐ GAG ME
- ☐ GROSS OUT

HOUSE OF CARDS

Teddy's uncle Pedro uses playing cards to hypnotize Nate. What's in the cards for you? See if you can find each of these playing-card terms in the puzzle on the opposite page.

SPADE

QUEEN

DIAMOND

CLUB

JOKER

ACE

DECK

HAND

LUCKY

FLUSH

GAME

CARD

HEART

KING

JACK

FULL HOUSE

CHANCE

DEAL

K	O	N	C	Y	J	H	B	O	K
C	C	L	K	C	S	O	D	E	I
N	E	C	L	U	B	N	K	H	N
F	U	L	L	H	O	U	S	E	G
L	K	F	H	M	H	N	N	A	R
D	C	H	A	N	C	E	M	R	D
D	E	I	J	L	A	E	I	T	N
E	D	A	P	S	R	U	O	H	A
J	C	L	L	U	D	Q	L	E	H
K	I	A	N	E	N	D	U	S	K

WHAP!! AWKWARD!

Nate and his friends always find themselves in sticky situations. List your TOP 20 most awkward moments!

1.

2.

TRIP!

3.

4.

5. Having toilet paper stuck to you

6.

7.

8. Throwing up in gym class

9.

10.

11.

12. Burping in math class

13.

14.

15.

16.

17.

18. Getting tangled in a jump rope

19.

20.

GINA GALLERY

Yearbook editor, teacher's pet, Nate's nemesis! Can you capture the many faces of Gina? Copy each Gina face in one of the blank boxes below.

GET SET, SCRIBBLE

**Can you play the scribble game
with your eyes <u>closed</u>?**

Open your eyes and write a caption.

YOUR OWN YEARBOOK

What if there was a yearbook all about <u>you</u>?
Obnoxious Gina would call hers The Ginacle.

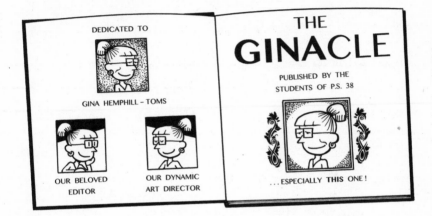

NOW DESIGN YOUR OWN COVER!

TITLE: _____

HIDEAWAY!

Nate jams in the garage with his band, Enslave the Mollusk. Where do you and your friends hang out? See if you can hunt down all these hideaways in the puzzle!

CORNER STORE

GYM

MUSIC ROOM

GAZEBO

LIBRARY

TENT

GAME ROOM

COMIC BOOK STORE

TREE HOUSE

BASEMENT

BUNK BED

GARAGE

ATTIC

FORT

FOREST

```
N T O F M R M R C E F R T T
R I B E O O T F O M S C B E
B G A M E R O O M G R U O T
C T C O T B R R I R N E R M
O O Y O E H A T C K Y E A S
G B R Z E E O N B I E S F R
C A A N R C C E O H S O G R
T G R B E R D T O A R U Y E
E B B A S R R U K E E T M O
A T I A G O S E S R T C O N
U S L T G E A T T I C T M S
E R I R K I E C O N C I T T
O T O Y T R O N R R O I O I
B O R R R B A S E M E N T O
```

...BEANBAG CHAIRS!

FLUMP!

ZONED OUT

What happens when Nate's boring science teacher is droning on? Or his sister is bragging again? He spaces out!
LIST your TOP 15 zoned-out moments!!

NOBODY LIKES A SHOW-OFF, SON. WHEN YOU CALL ATTENTION TO YOURSELF DURING CLASS, IT BEC BLAH BLAH BLAH BLAH BLAH BLA BLAH BLAH BLAH

1. You've been playing your favorite video game for hours!

2.

3. You're staring at your crush of 5 years.

4.

5.

6.

7.

8. You're in class. It's snowing outside, and you're dreaming of snowboarding.

9.

GROAN

10.

11.

12.

13. You ate too many Cheez Doodles—MUST HAVE MORE! They've fried your brain.

14.

15.

ELLEN IS A **JOY** TO TEACH!

NEVER HAVE I HAD SUCH A DEDICATED STUDENT!

HER SUNNY DISPOSITION **LIGHTS UP** THE CLASSROOM!

SHE'S AN **INSPIRATION** TO **EVERYONE** AROUND HER!

1,2,3...SNAP!

Solve the maze and find
the funniest photo of all!

START

FINISH

BEST FRIENDS FOREVER

Me and Francis in kindergarten

Nate and Francis have been best friends since they were little—they even have a secret code! Who's <u>your</u> best friend?

ALL ABOUT MY BFF

BFF's name: _____

Nickname: _____

Favorite song: _____

Pet's name: _____

Favorite color: _____

Hobby: _____

Best school subject: _____

Most loved food: _____

Favorite game ever: _____

NEAT FREAK

Nate's best friend Francis is so neat he color codes his underwear! What are your top 15 NEAT-FREAK moments? List them below, then rank them from 1 (tidy) to 10 (clean queen/king)!

NEAT-FREAK MOMENT	RANK
1.	____
2.	____
3.	____
4.	____
5. Dusting the closet	____
6.	____
7.	____
8. Alphabetizing my toys	____

9. _____

10. _____

11. _____

12. _____

13. Cleaning the inside of my gym shoes _____

14. _____

15. _____

ODD JOB-A-THON

Teddy's uncle Pedro has oodles of odd jobs. See if you can spot them in the puzzle on the opposite page. If you find all 11, you get a free palm reading!

ROOFER

LANDSCAPER

MUSICIAN

PALM READER

CARPENTER

SMALL-ENGINE REPAIRMAN

HYPNOTIST

HAIR DRESSER

KNIFE SHARPENER

YOGA INSTRUCTOR

LIVE-BAIT SALESMAN

```
N R I E N D A R I E Y I L I A Y C Y A S
A A C S S K K I R S E I T I C S O N A L
M U S I C I A N T C N R R R L G E C L L
S M A L L E N G I N E R E P A I R M A N
E R M S R R P S T F S P A I S H G N E S
L O E A R S R L O M E L N E N I D I A H
A H A A T N R O E A M S O C C S A M E P
S M Y V M I R S F R T U H N C N N S L T
T N O P R E S S E R D R I A H R A A E O
I A M T N T P A U N A T P P R N A R P U
A A E O N O D C F E S E I R E P P S N V
B E O P R E T N E P R A C R P H E G E E
E N I S R O I I S M E E E M I I D N E U
V R P R R N N R S A T S N P N R O E E N
I E R A E L A N O T R O R D I T C I E R
L A S N K R R R S S R I I E O S E A R D
```

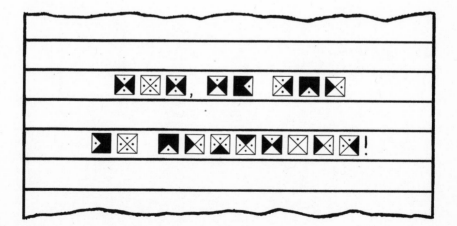

YEARBOOK LINEUP

Take control of The Chronicle and become yearbook editor. Match each kid to the right title.

MOST AWESOME

SMARTEST

BIGGEST ATHLETE

MOST LIKELY TO SUCCEED

MOST THEATRICAL

BIGGEST BULLY

NICEST CLASSMATE

ACE
PHOTOGRAPHER

Who takes the best photos at P.S. 38?

START

FINISH

REWARD ROUNDUP

Nate's dad rewards him with a hot fudge sundae when he cleans his room. List your TOP 20 REWARDS ever!

1. **A fluffy puppy!**	16.
2.	17.
3.	18. **a trip to the mall**
4.	19.
5.	20.
6. **jelly beans**	
7.	
8.	
9.	
10.	
11.	
12.	
13.	
14.	
15.	

I THINK WE SHOULD MAKE SOME HOT FUDGE SUNDAES!

NOW DRAW THE MOST AWESOME REWARD YOU'VE EVER RECEIVED!

WACKY COMIX

What happens when you combine Dee Dee, Uncle Pedro, and Randy the bully? Watch out, big-time drama!

  =

YOUR TITLE HERE

LUCKY CHARMS

Nate is superstitious. He believes in lucky charms. Fill in the grid so that each of these lucky charms shows up once in every row, column, and box!

P = **LUCKY PENNY**

R = **RABBIT'S FOOT**

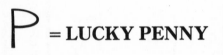

F = **FOUR-LEAF CLOVER**

H = **HORSESHOE**

MEGA-MESS

Nate needs to clean up his act! Can you find all the messy and gross items in the puzzle on the opposite page?

BANANA PEEL

DEAD BUGS

CANDY WRAPPERS

PENCIL SHAVINGS

STINKY SOCKS

EGG SALAD SANDWICH

MOLDY CHEESE

ROTTEN APPLE

KLEENEX

GYM SHORTS

HAIR GEL

OLD CHEWING GUM

S T R O H S M Y G M V D L R C A
T R X R A G I H E S H G E G S N
I Y E E D N R T G P D Y E H D G
N L N P I I C P Y S L H L S K A
K R E L P V U M D G I S S D A M
Y E E H H A I R G E L W A D M O
S U L R A H R S U K H N P E B L
O E K S E S S W T G N N S A B D
C H X H E L A T Y O D C N D I Y
K I C D N I P A D D H A E B A C
S P O L D C H E W I N G G U M H
H C I W D N A S D A L A S G G E
L R O T T E N A P P L E C S S E
E G E V P P S E E L N R Y S N S
N S V L S I E L D T C R T N S E
G B E C P L T E E C A K M D E A

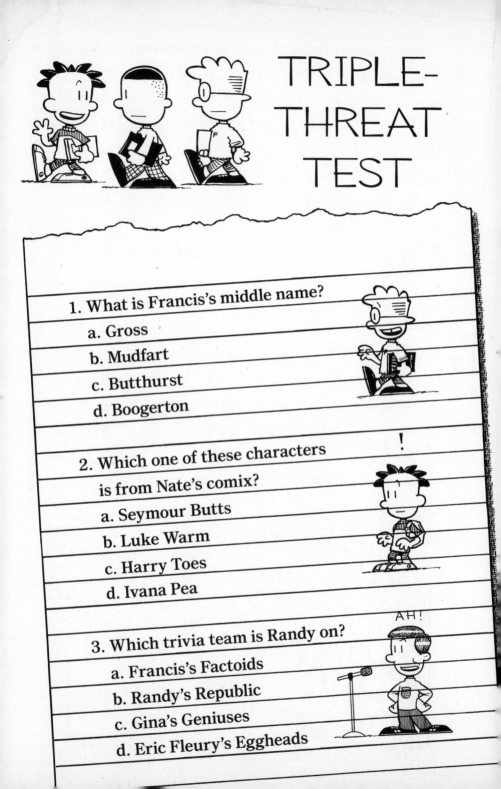

TRIPLE-THREAT TEST

1. What is Francis's middle name?

   a. Gross

   b. Mudfart

   c. Butthurst

   d. Boogerton

2. Which one of these characters is from Nate's comix?

   a. Seymour Butts

   b. Luke Warm

   c. Harry Toes

   d. Ivana Pea

3. Which trivia team is Randy on?

   a. Francis's Factoids

   b. Randy's Republic

   c. Gina's Geniuses

   d. Eric Fleury's Eggheads

4. What's Chad's superhero name?

   a. Champion Chad

   b. Chadtastic

   c. Charming Chad

   d. Mega-Chad

5. What is Dee Dee's last name?

   a. Popowski

   b. Pierce

   c. Applewhite

   d. Holloway

6. What kind of pet does Chad have?

   a. Kuddle Kitten

   b. gerbil

   c. parakeet

   d. turtle

NUTTY NICKNAMES

One of Nate's favorite hobbies is coming up with gross nicknames for his social studies teacher, Godzilla, aka Mrs. Godfrey. Match the words below to make more nicknames for Nate's list!

NUTTER	PARADE
CRAZY	STINKER
DEATH	GARGOYLE
SASSY	BUTT
MEAN	BREATH
LADY	DRAGON
MEGA	QUEEN
GREASY	BUTTER
CUCKOO	PANTS
DOOM	DUCHESS

WRITE YOUR TOP 10 NICKNAMES HERE.

1.
2.
3.
4.
5.
6.
7.
8.
9.
10.

CRAZY CHARACTERS

Put on your thinking cap and make new character names for each person or animal below! The crazier, the better!

LAUGH ATTACK

Teddy is the ultimate jokester. Use the code on page 9 to find out the punch lines!

Q: What has one head, one foot, and four legs?

A: ◪ ◩◪ ◪◪◩◪

_ _ _ _

Q: What sound do porcupines make when they kiss?

HEH HEH! MMPH! *SNORT!*

A: ◪◪◪◪!

_ _ _ _!

Q: What goes through towns and up hills but doesn't move?

A: ◪◪◪ ◪◪◪◪!

_ _ _ _ _ _ _!

GROUCHY GODFREY

Geez, Nate's least favorite teacher, Mrs. Godfrey, is ALWAYS grumpy! What's she growling about now? You decide. Fill in the bubbles!

QUICK DRAW!

Think fast! Draw a comic that includes
a pirate, Dee Dee, and Nate!

 +

  =

YOUR TITLE HERE

UNDERCOVER

Do you want to be an international spy or master of disguise, like Dee Dee? Draw lines from Column A to Column B below to create super-spy names!

Column A

DANGER

CAPTAIN

SPEEDY

DARK

SUPER

FLYING

SILVER

QUEEN

MASTER

AMAZING

SERGEANT

Column B

INVISIBLE

FLASH

RANGER

AWESOME

SQUIRREL

SPARROW

SENSATION

MYSTERY

FLY

DYNAMO

BOLT

WRITE YOUR TOP 10
SUPER-SPY NAMES HERE.

1.
2.
3.
4.
5.
6.
7.
8.
9.
10.

CAPTION ACTION

You've been made yearbook editor of P.S. 38! Come up with funny captions for each photo and fill in the blanks!

_____
_____
_____

_____
_____
_____

_____
_____
_____

_____

_____

_____

_____

_____

_____

_____

_____

_____

_____

_____

_____

DARE TO DREAM

When you go to sleep, do you have outrageously crazy dreams, like Nate? List the TOP 20 wildest things you dream about! Then rank them from 1 to 20.

DREAM	RANK
1. Starring in a movie	_____
2.	_____
3.	_____
4. Fighting aliens	_____
5.	_____
6.	_____
7.	_____
8. Becoming a superhero	_____

9. Throwing slime on the school bully _____

10. _____

11. Riding a dinosaur _____

12. _____

13. _____

14. Winning the
    Trivia Slam _____

15. _____

16. _____

17. Swimming in marshmallows _____

18. _____

19. Getting your own reality TV show _____

20. _____

SECRET CRUSH

Nate's always had a HUGE crush on his classmate Jenny!
Now you play matchmaker. Draw lines from Column A
to Column B and decide who makes the cutest couples.

COLUMN A

COLUMN B

PRIVATE EYE

Luke Warm is about to crack the case of the missing camera. Fill in the speech bubbles and solve the crime!

SCHOOL YARD COOL

Dee Dee loves to jump rope, and Teddy's the kickball king. What's at the top of your recess list? See if you can find all these awesome activities in the super search on the next page!

TETHERBALL

HOPSCOTCH

WALL BALL

LEAPFROG

HIDE-AND-SEEK

MONKEY BARS

TIRE SWING

FREEZE TAG

SLIDE

JUNGLE GYM

SOCCER

FOUR SQUARE

PARACHUTE

KICKBALL

> GINA! WANT TO JUMP ROPE IN THE SCHOOL YARD?

> OKAY!

GINA
THE GREAT

Gina knows just how to annoy Nate BIG-time! How well do you know Gina? See if you can ace this quiz! True or false?

1. Gina plays drums in Nate's band.

☐ TRUE   ☐ FALSE

2. Nate's had a crush on Gina since first grade.

WHA-?

☐ TRUE   ☐ FALSE

3. Gina's the editor of the yearbook.

HERE'S WHAT I'VE DONE!

☐ TRUE   ☐ FALSE

4. Gina named Nate's fleeceball team the Kuddle Kittens.

STRIKE ONE!

☐ TRUE   ☐ FALSE

5. Mrs. Godfrey is Gina's favorite teacher.

☐ TRUE   ☐ FALSE

6. Artur is dating Gina.

☐ TRUE   ☐ FALSE

GAWK!

BUBBLE TROUBLE

What is each character saying?? Fill in the speech bubbles as FAST as you can and create the fun!

SPLURCH!

NATE FACE-OFF!

Can you copy Nate's many faces? Go for it!

WHOSE LOCKER IS IT?

Nate is known for being SUPER messy, and his best friend Francis is a total neat freak. Which locker item is Nate's and which one belongs to Francis?

COLUMN A

SWEATY SOCKS

APPLE

TRIVIA BOOK

CHEEZ DOODLES

GROSS GYM SHORTS

TOOTHBRUSH

MR. GALVIN'S DENTURES

MATH HOMEWORK

CALCULATOR

MOLDY MOUTHGUARD

HEAD OF A LAWN GNOME

NAPKINS

SUNSCREEN

OLD TURKEY SANDWICH

COLUMN B

NATE

FRANCIS

NATE-TASTIC TRIVIA

OH! THAT REMINDS ME!...

Quick! Find out if you're the master of Nate-knowledge! Circle the right answer.

I CAN'T BELIEVE IT!

1. When Nate is hypnotized, how does he change?

YOU'RE LIKE A DIFFERENT PERSON!

a. He starts wearing superhero costumes.

b. He becomes neat.

c. He becomes yearbook editor.

d. He dates Jenny (finally!).

2. Who's the toughest hall monitor ever?

IT'S SO OBVIOUS!

a. Gina Hemphill-Toms

b. Nick Blonsky

c. Francis

d. Randy Betancourt

3. What is the middle name of Nate's dramatic
friend, Dee Dee?

a. Butthurst

b. Mud

c. Dorcas

d. Speaker

4. Who hypnotized Nate?

a. Mrs. Godfrey

b. Gina

c. Uncle Pedro

d. Jenny

5. Nate's favorite sport is . . .

a. basketball

b. Jazzercise

c. hockey

d. fleeceball

I JUST... **NOTICED** IT, THAT'S ALL!

STOP, DROP, AND DRAW!

Ready? Pick up that pencil!! Create a super-cool comic using these characters.

 +

+ =

YOUR TITLE HERE

DETECTIVE DEE DEE

Dee Dee LOVES to solve school mysteries at P.S. 38! See if you can become a super sleuth too. Find all 15 words hidden in the puzzle!

SPY

SCENE

PRIVATE EYE

MYSTERY

HIDDEN

SPECIAL AGENT

EVIDENCE

SUSPECT

MAGNIFYING GLASS

INVESTIGATE

CRIME

SECRET

TRANCE

POLICE

CASE

SCRIBBLE
STATION

What will you turn your scribble into?

Don't forget to write a caption:

SNACK-TASTIC!

Chad goes mad for donuts, Nate is crazy for Cheez Doodles, and Dee Dee loves cinnamon buns. What about you? Rank these snacks from 1 to 10. 1 is just yum, and 10 is TOTALLY DELICIOUS!

SNACK	RANK
1. Gummy bears	___
2. Chocolate-chip cookies	___
3. Jelly beans	___
4. Mixed nuts	___
5. Crackers	___
6. String cheese	___
7. Apples and peanut butter	___
8. Raisins	___

9. Yogurt _____

10. Granola bar _____

11. Popcorn _____

12. Pretzels _____

13. Baby carrots _____

14. Cheez Doodles _____

15. Banana _____

URK!

And what's the GROSSEST thing you've ever eaten?

Our chocolate-chip coffee cake is **DONE**! Time for a **TASTE TEST**!

YAAAAAY!!

COPY SHOP

Quick! Put your cartooning skills to the test! Try drawing each of these characters in the blank boxes below.

DAD DRAMA

Nate is one troublemaker who definitely drives his dad crazy! What do you do that makes your dad insane?

LIST YOUR TOP 20 HERE!

1.

2. Skateboarding in the dining room

3.

4.

5.

6.

7.

8. Picking your nose

9.

10.

11. Eating only potato chips for dinner

12.

13.

NATE... IS THERE ANYTHING YOU WANT TO TELL ME?

14. Dressing up the neighbor's cat

15.

16.

17. Putting worms in your sister's hair

KA-WANG!

18.

19. Leaving dirty socks everywhere

20.

!

Watch out, Nate's in trouble big-time. Fill in the speech bubbles and decide what they're yelling about! Then give each comic a crazy title.

WRITE YOUR TITLE HERE!

ROCKIN' OUT

Nate, Teddy, Artur, and Francis have their own band—Enslave the Mollusk!

What's your favorite band or pop star?

Name their best song:

What does the band wear onstage?

Name the #1 reason they're awesome!

NOW DRAW YOUR BAND PERFORMING FOR A HUGE CROWD!

DANCE FEVER

Can you bust a move like Nate and Dee Dee? See if you can find all the different dances in this hidden-word puzzle. Then join the dance party!

POLKA

HIP-HOP

BALLET

BREAK DANCE

HOKEY POKEY

TAP

SWING

FLAMENCO

MODERN

BELLY DANCE

JAZZ

SALSA

TANGO

DISCO

BALLROOM

WALTZ

HULA

TWIST

S	A	N	C	K	O	R	B	E	A	A
E	L	M	L	I	Y	G	N	I	W	S
A	C	O	C	N	E	M	A	L	F	L
E	C	N	A	D	K	A	E	R	B	A
D	T	R	A	P	O	L	K	A	N	S
I	W	E	N	D	P	G	L	Z	H	W
S	I	D	O	A	Y	L	N	I	N	A
C	S	O	T	H	E	L	P	A	L	L
O	T	M	U	T	K	H	L	A	T	T
B	A	L	L	R	O	O	M	E	K	Z
J	A	Z	Z	P	H	K	G	P	B	O

TALENT TIME

Nate's friend Teddy has a special trick—he can make fart noises with his armpit! What other weird talents do you think the kids at P.S. 38 have? Write them down next to each name!

Nate: _____

Chester: _Blows yogurt out his nose_____

Dee Dee: _____

Gina: _____

Francis: _____

Teddy: _Armpit fart_____

Jenny: _____

Artur: _____

Chad: _____

NAME YOUR TALENT! ➜

You: _____

REALLY? AWESOME!

EDITOR-IN-CHIEF

Who should be the editor of the Chronicle?

HOOP IT UP!

Nate's got some skills on the basketball court. Check out his jump shot! Let's see what you can do. Using the letters in "basketball," see how many words you can create!

BASKETBALL

1.
2.
3.
4.
5.
6.
7.
8.
9.
10.
11.
12.
13.
14.

15.

16.

17.

18.

19.

20.

DRAMATIC FLASHBACK!

What happened before?
It's up to you! Draw it.

HOW DID NATE MAKE THIS MESS?

WHO HIT PRINCIPAL NICHOLS?

UH-OH! WHAT DID NATE DO NOW?

WHAT IS DEE DEE UP TO?

WHO THREW THE BOTTLE?

ANGER DANGER

Nate's up to his old tricks! How mad are his teachers now? Draw a line from each teacher to the right level on the rage meter.

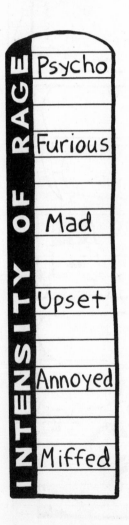

INTENSITY OF RAGE

- Psycho
- Furious
- Mad
- Upset
- Annoyed
- Miffed

ULTRA-NATE AND MEGA-CHAD

These two are the ultimate team of superheroes!
Fill in the speech bubbles and help them save Maya!

LUCKY CHARMS

Chad has a special plastic foot that he carries with him for good luck. What's your lucky charm? Draw it!

NOW UNSCRAMBLE THE WORDS BELOW
TO FIND MORE GOOD-LUCK CHARMS!

V R E C L O _ _ _ _ _ _

(Clue: green; picked by leprechauns)

A R B B T I _ _ _ _ _ _

T O F O _ _ _ _

(Clue: bunny paw)

IT'S PART OF SOME SORT OF **ACTION FIGURE!**

O S R H E S O H E _ _ _ _ _ _ _ _ _

(Clue: bigger than a pony; footwear)

R S A T _ _ _ _

(Clue: Shines brightly!)

RIGHT AFTER YOU LEFT FOR THE PRINCIPAL'S OFFICE, I FOUND IT ON THE FLOOR OF THE CAFETORIUM!

A I B R O W N _ _ _ _ _ _ _

(Clue: There's a pot of gold at the end!)

BOOK NOOK

Nate spends a lot of time in the library, even though the librarian, Mrs. Hickson, is not his biggest fan! What about you?

QUICK QUIZ:

1. What is your favorite book?

2. Who's the character that you like best?

3. If you gave the book a new title, what would it be?

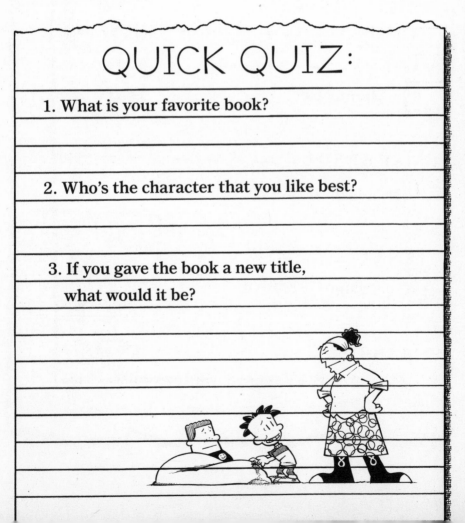

4. If you could create a new cover for the book, what would it look like?

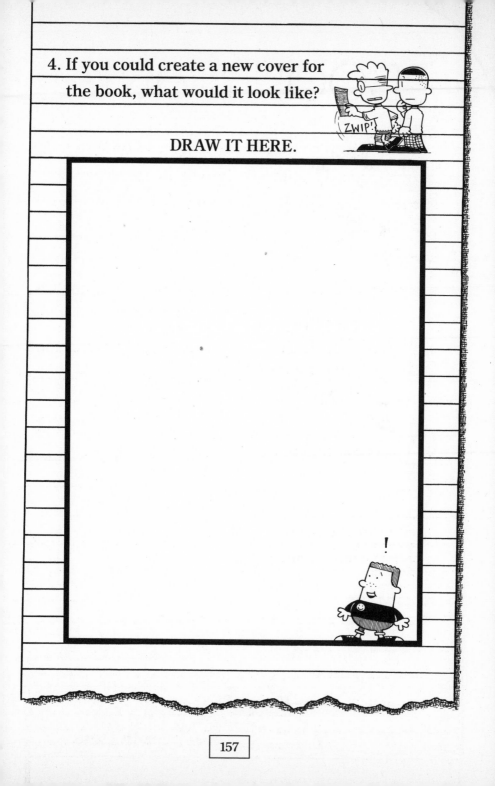

DRAW IT HERE.

DOODLEMANIA!

Nate fills his whole notebook with doodles—how about you? We dare you!

MR. PERFECT

Annoyingly perfect Artur has joined Nate's band! What will happen next? Fill in the speech bubbles, and fast!

LOVE FEST

Teddy loves sports,
Nate loves comix,
and Artur loves Jenny!

WHICH OF THESE THINGS DO YOU LOVE MOST? RATE THEM FROM 1 (HO-HUM) TO 10 (INFATUATION).

	RATING
· Pizza party	_____
· Playing with your pet	_____
· Ice cream sundaes	_____
· Ping Pong	_____
· Amusement park	_____
· Skateboarding	_____
· Board games	_____
· Jelly beans	_____

ROWR! HEE HEE!
WOOF!
WORF!

- Trick-or-treating　———

- Pajama Day at school　———

- Camping　———

- Flying a kite　———

- Building a sand castle　———

- Jumping on your bed　———

- Visiting your grandparent　———

- Playing baseball　———

- Dancing　———

- Peanut butter and jelly sandwiches　———

- Swimming in the ocean　———

- Climbing a tree　———

COMIX CAPTAIN

Create your own comic using Chad,
a saber-toothed swamp cat, and Coach John!

 +

+ =

?

YOUR TITLE HERE

ON THE SPOT

Are you the master of Nate knowledge? Prove it! Do you think these statements are true or false?

1. Nate loves Jazzercise.

☐ TRUE ☐ FALSE

2. Stuffed cabbage is Chad's favorite meal.

☐ TRUE ☐ FALSE

3. Mrs. Godfrey is Nate's favorite teacher.

☐ TRUE ☐ FALSE

4. Chad likes Maya.

☐ TRUE ☐ FALSE

5. Artur is the lead singer in Nate's band.

☐ TRUE ☐ FALSE

6. Dee Dee is really shy.

☐ TRUE ☐ FALSE

7. Chad's lucky charm is a plastic foot.

☐ TRUE ☐ FALSE

8. Nate's dad is dating Mrs. Godfrey.

☐ TRUE ☐ FALSE

9. Francis plays the guitar.

☐ TRUE ☐ FALSE

10. Teddy's uncle hypnotizes people.

☐ TRUE ☐ FALSE

11. Gina is Nate's best friend.

WHA-?...
☆SPUTTER!☆

☐ TRUE ☐ FALSE

MMM, GOOD!

Chad loves the smell of Ms. Brindle's class because it always smells like cinnamon!

NAME YOUR TOP 15 BEST SMELLS EVER:

1.
2.
3.
4. blueberry pancakes
5.
6.
7. chocolate cupcakes
8.
9. roses
10.
11.
12.
13.
14.
15.

MORNING MADNESS

Oh no, Claude, the stupid ideas fairy, visited Teddy for breakfast! Is disaster about to happen? You decide.

FAST-FORWARD

Can you tell the future? You decide what happens after each scene, then draw it!

MASTERMIND

POP QUIZ! CLEAR YOUR DESKS!

URK!

Pop quiz time! Don't sweat it—you've got this. Test your Nate trivia now!

1. Chad is covered in . . .

    a. sprinkles

    b. chicken pox

    c. beanbag pellets

    d. dirt

2. The nicest teacher at P.S. 38 is . . .

    a. Mrs. Godfrey

    b. Mr. Staples

    c. Coach John

    d. Mr. Rosa

GET A MOVE ON, SCRUBS! DOUBLE-TIME! HUP! HUP! HUP!

3. Nate's two best friends are . . .
   a. Randy and Marcus
   b. Francis and Teddy
   c. Maya and Dee Dee
   d. Spitsy and Pickles

4. Who's the biggest bully?
   a. Mr. Galvin
   b. Randy
   c. Marcus
   d. Pickles

HYPNOSIS CENTRAL

Where should Nate go to get hypnotized?

DETENTION PREVENTION

Principal Nichols has CANCELED Nate's detention!

List all the fun things Nate's going to do now!

1.
2. Eat cookies
3.
4.
5.
6. Play fleeceball
7.
8.
9.
10.
11.
12.
13. Tease Gina
14.
15.
16.
17.
18. Walk Spitsy
19.
20.

...I'LL HAVE TO **CANCEL** YOUR **DETENTION!**

BAND AID

Help Nate's band write some new songs for their next show! Fill in the blanks!

We're here to _____ ,

It's time to _____ ,

The beat is _____ on _____ ,

Just hear our _____ ,

The crowd goes _____ ,

For you, _____ child _____ ,

Hey, P.S. ____thirty-eight____,

You know you're _____,

Just like _____,

'Cause he's our _____,

He's super ____fly____,

Oh yeah, we _____,

We're here to _____!

HERE NOW, TO TELL YOU ALL ABOUT IT IN AN ORIGINAL SONG, IS P.S. 38's VERY OWN...

ENSLAVE THE MOLLUSK!

YAAAAY!

COMIX BY U!

Get ready! Create a comic using Principal Nichols, Nate, and a plastic bottle. I smell trouble!

 +

+ =

?

YOUR TITLE HERE

WOW WORDS

Nate has one very cool spot in the library—the beanbag chairs! Using the letters in the words "beanbag chair," see if you can make more than 20 other words!

BEANBAG CHAIR

1.	12.
2.	13.
3.	14.
4.	15.
5.	16.
6.	17.
7.	18.
8.	19.
9.	20.
10.	21.
11.	22.

MUSIC MAN

Chad plays oboe in the school band at P.S. 38.

DO YOU PLAY AN INSTRUMENT? WHICH ONE?

DRAW IT HERE!

NOW SEE IF YOU CAN FIND ALL THE DIFFERENT INSTRUMENTS IN THIS HIDDEN-WORD PUZZLE!

DRUM

TROMBONE

HARP

CLARINET

FLUTE

GUITAR

SAXOPHONE

PICCOLO

TRIANGLE

CYMBALS

VIOLA

TRUMPET

TUBA

FRENCH HORN

PIANO

OBOE

VIOLIN

BASS

T	C	T	E	P	M	U	R	T	H	L	M
O	A	I	N	N	G	R	P	U	C	M	N
N	I	L	O	I	V	I	P	O	U	G	N
N	R	O	H	H	C	N	E	R	F	I	B
M	P	B	P	C	A	O	D	O	T	Y	F
L	T	R	O	M	B	O	N	E	B	I	L
I	A	L	X	G	P	O	N	L	P	O	U
H	O	S	A	S	U	I	O	E	A	A	T
C	I	A	S	T	R	I	A	N	G	L	E
C	Y	M	B	A	L	S	T	N	F	O	N
C	A	G	L	U	B	T	O	A	O	I	N
I	A	C	I	B	T	C	A	L	R	V	L

**BONUS QUESTION: IF YOU COULD PLAY
ANY INSTRUMENT IN THE WORLD,
WHAT WOULD IT BE?**

GAME ON!

Nate and Chad are in the middle of a heated hockey game in gym class. Using the letters in the words "hockey stick," see if you can create more than 20 other words and help Nate win the game!

HOCKEY STICK

1.	15.
2.	16.
3.	17.
4. yoke	18.
5.	19. key
6.	20.
7.	21.
8.	22.
9.	
10.	
11.	
12.	
13. kick	
14.	

ARE YOU A HOCKEY CHAMP, LIKE NATE?

☐ YES   ☐ NO

LET'S SEE YOUR SKILLS!
DRAW A PICTURE OF YOURSELF
PLAYING HOCKEY HERE!

COMIX CONNECTION

It's time for an awesome comix connection!
Draw a comic using Chad and Maya—
show how they first meet!

YOUR TITLE HERE

SIBLING RIVALRY

Me and Ellen

Do you have a brother or sister? Nate's older sister, Ellen, can be a serious pain sometimes!

LIST THE TOP 10 THINGS YOUR BROTHER OR SISTER DOES THAT ANNOY YOU.

WE'RE GETTING BACK OUR BOOK REPORTS, WHICH I KNOW I DID WELL ON! AND I'M TRYING OUT FOR THE SCHOOL MUSICAL! AND I'M RUNNING FOR CLASS PRESIDENT! AND THEN...

1.

2.

3. Eats all the cereal.

4.

5.

6.

7.

8. Uses my stuff without asking!

9.

10.

NATE WAS TALKING TO A GIRRRL!

KISS KISS KISSY KISS

NOW, WHAT ARE THE TOP 10 THINGS
YOU LOVE ABOUT YOUR BROTHER
OR SISTER?

1.

2.

3.

4.

5.

6.

7.

8.

9.

10.

DRAW A PICTURE OF YOU
WITH YOUR SIBLINGS!

FUNNY BONE

Teddy is one funny jokester! Using his secret code below, figure out the punch lines to Teddy's seriously silly jokes.

A	B	C	D	E	F	G	H	I	J	K	L	M
Z	Y	X	W	V	U	T	S	R	Q	P	O	N

N	O	P	Q	R	S	T	U	V	W	X	Y	Z
M	L	K	J	I	H	G	F	E	D	C	B	A

Q: Why did the picture go to jail?

A: __ __ __ __ __ __ __ __ __
Y V X Z F H V   R G

__ __ __ __ __ __ __ __ .
D Z H   U I Z N V W

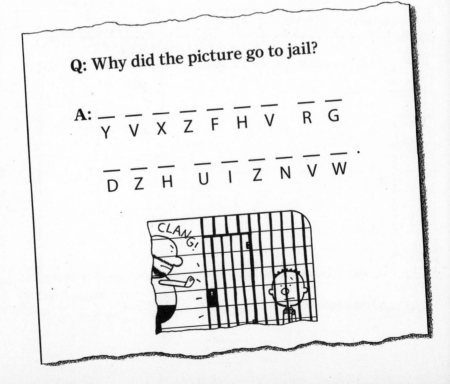

CLANG!

Q: What did the paper say to the pencil?

A: $\underline{}\ \underline{}\ \underline{}\ \underline{}\ \underline{}\ \underline{}\ \underline{}$!
  D I R G V L M

Q: Why was the broom late?

A: $\underline{}\ \underline{}\ \underline{}\ \underline{}\ \underline{}\ \underline{}\ \underline{}\ \underline{}\ \underline{}\ \underline{}\ \underline{}$!
  R G L E V I H D V K G

Q: What goes up and down but does not move?

A: $\underline{}\ \underline{}\ \underline{}\ \underline{}\ \underline{}\ \underline{}$.
  H G Z R I H

Q: How do you make a walnut laugh?

A: $\underline{}\ \underline{}\ \underline{}\ \underline{}\ \underline{}\ \underline{}\ \underline{}\ \underline{}\ \underline{}$!
  X I Z X P R G F K

GODZILLA

Who's Nate's scariest teacher, nicknamed Godzilla? Mrs. Godfrey! For each letter in her name, write down an adjective or phrase that describes her, beginning with that letter. Do it before you get detention!

M_____

R_____

S cary_____

.

G_____

O_____

D_____

F_____

R_____

E_____

Y_____

STAGE FRIGHT

DURING MY THIRD-GRADE PRODUCTION OF "ALICE IN WONDERLAND," I FORGOT **ALL MY LINES!**

I JUST **STOOD** THERE SAYING **NOTHING!**

When Dee Dee was in "Alice in Wonderland," she forgot her lines and just stood there saying NOTHING!

LIST YOUR TOP 10 STAGE FRIGHT FREAK-OUTS.

1.
2.
3.
4.
5.
6.
7. There was toilet paper stuck to my costume!
8.
9.
10.

SCHOOL STORY

Nate's school, P.S. 38, is pretty cool—the mascot is the Bobcat; there's the Doodlers, their cartooning club; and they play fleeceball!

What's your school story?

YOUR SCHOOL NAME:

_____

MASCOT:

_____

SCHOOL COLORS:

_____

FSST!

I'M THE P.S. 38 *BOBCAT!*

ROWR!

CLUBS YOU BELONG TO:

_____

FAVORITE TEACHER:

_____

MOST EXCITING AFTER-SCHOOL EVENT:

_____

BIGGEST RIVAL SCHOOL:

_____

**BEST PERFORMANCE
(GAME, PLAY, CONCERT):**

_____

REPLICATION NATION

Are you a super cartoonist? Let's see your talent!

Copy each Big Nate drawing in the boxes below!

WORST WEEK EVER!

Nate is having one very bad week—check out his lowlights! Ugh, cavities AND a pink uniform? Describe your WORST WEEK EVER, one day at a time:

MONDAY:

TUESDAY:

WEDNESDAY:

THURSDAY:

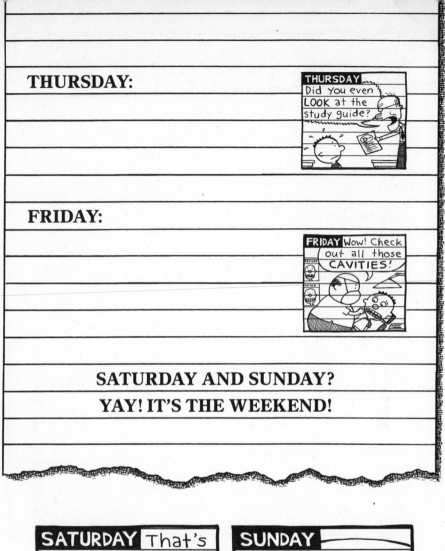

FRIDAY:

SATURDAY AND SUNDAY?

YAY! IT'S THE WEEKEND!

TRENDSETTER

THUNK THUNK
THUNK THUNK
THUNK THUNK
THUNK THUNK

Nate's started some fun and kind of wacky trends at his school, like hitting his head with a plastic bottle and doodling on his sneakers.

DRAW YOUR FAVORITE TRENDS:

COOLEST SNEAKERS

OOOOH! NATE!

YOUR SHOES ARE FABULOUS!

CRAZIEST HAIRSTYLE

BEST NEW ACCESSORY

MOST AWESOME OUTFIT

TAKE A SHOT!

Coach John is the master of basketball. He's challenging Nate to make one tough shot. Can he do it? Solve the puzzle and help Nate make a basket!

CLUES

ACROSS

5. Circular, rhymes with "soup."

6. Take a _____! Rhymes with "hot."

7. A basketball word for "bounce." Rhymes with "nibble."

DOWN

1. Rhymes with "lump." This makes you shoot higher!

2. This could also be where the Easter Bunny puts his eggs.

3. A fish might get caught in this.

4. Where the game is played; this has wood floors.

8. Rhymes with "hall." Shoot it!

SHOOFF!

BIRD FOOD

Nate can't handle it! They're replacing all the snacks in the school vending machine with "bird food." Ugh!

LIST THE TOP 20 WORST SNACKS HERE!

1.
2.
3.
4. broccoli
5.
6.
7.
8.
9. kale chips
10.
11.
12.

13.	
14.	
15.	sunflower seeds
16.	
17.	
18.	
19.	
20.	

ANSWER KEY

POP QUIZ PARTY! (pp. 1–2)
1. (b) Kim Cressly
2. (d) Nick Blonsky
3. (c) flute
4. (c) Gina's Geniuses
5. (d) get a C on his homework
Bonus Points! (c) neat
Semaphore: Will you get an A?

WALK THE PLANK (pp. 6–7)

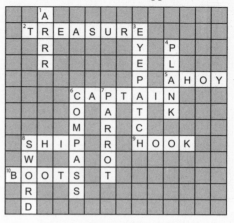

NAME THAT BRAIN! (p. 8)

DRESS TO IMPRESS (pp. 14–15)

SLAM DUNK (p. 12)

SHORTCUT! (p. 22)
Semaphore: Run, Nate!

PROBLEM PICS (p.23)

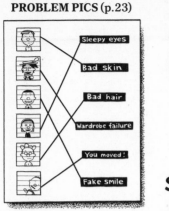

- Sleepy eyes
- Bad skin
- Bad hair
- Wardrobe failure
- You moved!
- Fake smile

YOU'RE AN ACE! (pp. 26–27)

S	H	D	C
D	C	H	S
C	D	S	H
H	S	C	D

MASTERMIND MATCHUP (p. 28)

Semaphore: Who will win?

COME **STRAIGHT HOME** AFTER SCHOOL!

FACTASTIC FRANCIS (pp. 30–31)

1. (c) learning new trivia
2. (d) Captain Tidypants
3. (c) cat
4. (d) no siblings. He's an only child.
5. (b) ironing his tube socks
6. (b) an epidemiologist

KNOCKOUT NOTES (pp. 32–33)

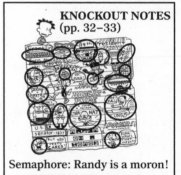

Semaphore: Randy is a moron!

GUESS WHO? (pp. 34–35)

Across/Down answers:
- P (PICCA...)
- ARTUR
- FRANCIS
- GINA
- JENNY
- ELLEN
- DEEDEE
- TEDDY
- MR ROSA
- MRS GODFREY

SUPER SPY (p. 36)

START
FINISH
KSSSSCHH!

THINKING CAPS (pp. 42–43)

BRAIN BOWL
(pp. 44–45)
1. North America
2. Spider
3. Saturn
4. Butterfly
5. Japan
6. Heart
7. Triangle
8. Oxygen
9. Atlantic, Pacific, Indian, Arctic, Southern
10. New York

FUNKY FITNESS
(pp. 46–47)

D	M	C	F
C	F	M	D
F	C	D	M
M	D	F	C

NATE NERD
(pp. 48–49)

1. True 3. False 5. False
2. False 4. True 6. True

ROOM RAID (pp. 52–53)

Semaphore: Watch out!

IT'S A WONDERFUL LIFE (p. 55)

SCHOOL SCRAMBLE (p. 54)

PASS THAT CLASS!
(pp. 56–57)
1. (c) Timber Scouts
2. (d) Nick Blonsky
3. (b) Uncle Pedro
4. (d) Dee Dee
Extra Credit!
(b) Mr. McTeague
Semaphore:
Get a life, Gina!

READY, SET, CLICK!
(pp. 58–59)

FRANCIS FACTOIDS
(p. 62–63)

C	T	S	O	N	A
O	A	N	S	C	T
N	O	C	A	T	S
T	S	A	N	O	C
A	C	O	T	S	N
S	N	T	C	A	O

WHO'S WHO? (p. 65)

ERIC FLEURY
MARY ELLEN POPOWSKI
RANDY BETANCOURT
TEDDY ORTIZ
DEE DEE HOLLOWAY
GINA HEMPHILL-TOMS
FRANCIS POPE
CHAD APPLEWHITE
GIRL WHO DRAWS UNICORNS

CHEEZ, PLEASE!
(pp. 68–69)

HOUSE OF CARDS
(pp. 72–73)

Semaphore:
Lucky you!

AWKWARD!
(pp. 74–75)
Semaphore:
Uh-oh!

HIDEAWAY! (pp. 80–81)

1, 2, 3 . . . SNAP! (p. 84)

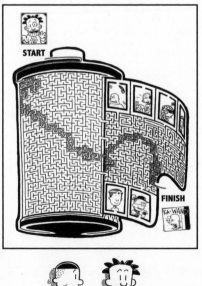

ODD JOB-A-THON (pp. 88–89)

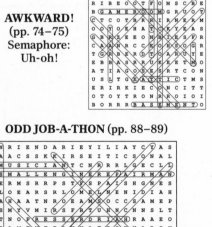

Semaphore: Wow, he can do anything!

YEARBOOK LINEUP (p. 90)

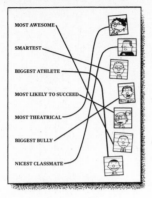

MOST AWESOME
SMARTEST
BIGGEST ATHLETE
MOST LIKELY TO SUCCEED
MOST THEATRICAL
BIGGEST BULLY
NICEST CLASSMATE

ACE PHOTOGRAPHER (p. 91)

START

FINISH

LUCKY CHARMS (pp. 96–97)

R	H	P	F
P	F	H	R
F	P	R	H
H	R	F	P

MEGA-MESS (pp. 98–99)

TRIPLE-THREAT TEST (pp. 100–101)

1. (c) Butthurst
2. (b) Luke Warm
3. (c) Gina's Geniuses
4. (d) Mega-Chad
5. (d) Holloway
6. (c) parakeet

LAUGH ATTACK (p. 106)

Semaphores: A bed
Ouch!
The road!

SCHOOL YARD COOL (pp. 118–119)

GINA THE GREAT
(pp. 120–121)

1. False   4. True
2. False   5. True
3. True   6. False

NATE-TASTIC TRIVIA
(pp. 126–127)

1. (b) He becomes neat.
2. (b) Nick Blonsky
3. (c) Dorcas
4. (c) Uncle Pedro
5. (d) fleeceball

WHOSE LOCKER IS IT?
(p. 125)

DETECTIVE DEE DEE
(pp. 130–131)

DAD DRAMA
(pp. 138–139)
Semaphore:
So bad!

DANCE FEVER
(pp. 144–145)

EDITOR-IN-CHIEF (p. 147)

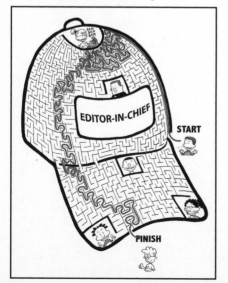

HOOP IT UP! (pp. 148–149)
Semaphore: Watch out, air ball!

ANGER DANGER (p.152)

LUCKY CHARMS
(pp. 154–155)
Clover
Rabbit foot
Horseshoe
Star
Rainbow

ON THE SPOT
(pp. 164–165)
1. False	7. True
2. False	8. False
3. False	9. True
4. True	10. True
5. True	11. False
6. False	

MASTERMIND
(pp. 170–171)
1. (c) beanbag pellets
2. (d) Mr. Rosa
3. (b) Francis and Teddy
4. (b) Randy

HYPNOSIS CENTRAL (p. 172)

MUSIC MAN (pp. 179–181)

FUNNY BONE (pp. 188–189)
Because it was framed.
Write on!
It overswept!
Stairs.
Crack it up!

TAKE A SHOT! (pp. 202–203)

			J				
			U		B		N
	C	M		A		E
H	O	O	P		S	H	O	T
	U			K	
D	R	I	B	B	L	E
	T		A	T	
			L	
			L	

LIVIN' LARGE!

P.S. 38 is pretty small. Everyone knows everyone else. So whenever a new kid shows up, it's a major event. Especially when he's got a name like **THIS**:

Boys and girls, this is Breckenridge Puffington III !

Anyway, Principal Nichols asked me to be the kid's "buddy," so it's my job to help him make friends...

MOVE it, Puff-ball!

SHOVE!

... and to show him around the school, which is falling apart. That's what happens when a building is one hundred years old.

CLONK!

OW!

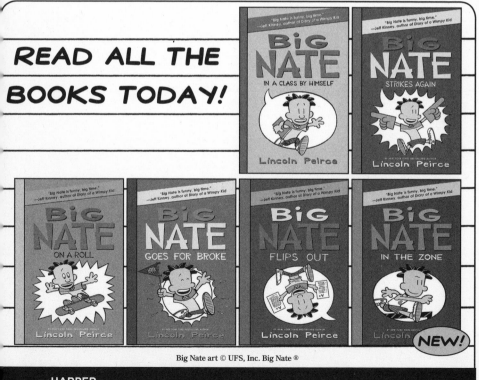